# Madame LaGrande
# and Her So High,
# To the Sky,
# Uproarious Pompadour

### by Candace Fleming

### illustrated by S. D. Schindler

Alfred A. Knopf
New York

*For Lynn, who read the words, and Anne, who laughed at them —C.F.*

*To Susan, who also likes cats in her hair —S.D.S.*

THIS IS A BORZOI BOOK PUBLISHED BY ALFRED A. KNOPF, INC.

Text copyright © 1996 by Candace Fleming
Illustrations copyright © 1996 by Steven D. Schindler

All rights reserved under International and Pan-American Copyright Conventions. Published in the United States of America
by Alfred A. Knopf, Inc., New York, and simultaneously in Canada by Random House of Canada Limited, Toronto.
Distributed by Random House, Inc., New York.

Manufactured in Singapore

Hand-lettering by Bernard Maisner

*Library of Congress Cataloging-in-Publication Data*
Fleming, Candace.
Madame LaGrande and her so high, to the sky, uproarious pompadour / by Candace Fleming ;
illustrated by Steven D. Schindler.
p. cm.
Summary: Madame LaGrande strives to be the most fashionable lady in Paris, but when her hairdresser
creates a spectacular pompadour for her, the results are disastrous.
[1. Hair — Fiction. 2. Paris (France) — Fiction. 3. Humorous stories.] I. Schindler,
S. D., ill. II. Title.
PZ7.F599936Mad 1996
[E]—dc20     94-42073

ISBN 0-679-85835-0 (trade)
ISBN 0-679-95835-5 (lib. bdg.)

10 9 8 7 6 5 4 3 2 1

𝒫oor Madame LaGrande. She tried so hard to be stylish. She spent long hours at the dressmaker. She wasted thousands of francs on hats, hairdos, and handbags. She read all the fashion magazines from cover to cover. Still, Madame LaGrande didn't have the fashion sense of a mule.

"I just haven't found the right style for me," she would often declare.

Then one day, as Madame flipped through the pages of her latest fashion magazine, a story caught her eye.

"Pompadours," she read, "are Paris's newest craze. These charming hairdos raise the hair several inches atop the head and are heavily powdered and intricately curled for a stylish effect."

Madame LaGrande read the story once. She read it twice. She leapt to her feet, squeezed into shoes three sizes too small, and rushed to Marcel's House of Hair Design.

"Ah, madame," gushed Marcel when he saw his best customer come through the door. "What triumph of hair design can I create for you today?"

"I want a pompadour," replied Madame. "A spectacular, magnificent pompadour such as Paris has never seen before. And I want to wear it to the Royal Opera tonight. Can you do it?"

"Oui, oui. But of course," nodded Marcel. "It will be perfection."

All afternoon, Marcel curled and crimped.
He powdered and primped.
He shaped and snipped.
And with the help of pillows and padding, wires and wigs, and the tallest ladder he could find, Marcel created an absolutely stupendous pompadour.

The hairdo stood so high atop Madame LaGrande's head that it almost touched the ceiling. Every inch of wig, wire, and pillow glistened with thick white powder. Throughout the towering tresses, Marcel had entwined ripening grapes still on the vine. And over each of Madame's ears hung a corkscrew curl.

"Voilà!" said Marcel with a flourish.

Madame looked at herself in the mirror. "Marcel, you are a genius," she said, patting the back of her head.

But when Madame stood, her hair was higher than the ceiling. She had to bow her head to get out the door. Once outside, she twisted and turned, trying to squeeze the tremendous hairdo into her waiting carriage. But it simply wouldn't fit. Madame had no choice but to walk to the Royal Opera.

On the boulevard, Madame passed a café where two plump pigeons searched for breadcrumbs beneath the tables. The pigeons spied the grapes in Madame's pompadour. They flew up. They perched atop the pompadour. They pecked at the fruit.

"Preposterous!"

"Ridiculous!"

"Absurd!" cried the café's customers.

Madame didn't notice the two plump pigeons pecking in her pompadour. She didn't notice the cries coming from the café. She noticed only that all eyes were upon her.

"They simply adore my hair," she said to herself. And she continued to the opera, holding her head even higher.

Three calico cats crouching on a window ledge saw the two plump pigeons pecking in Madame's pompadour. They flicked their tails. They licked their chops. They sprang!

The calico cats' claws caught in Madame's pompadour.
The cats began to yowl.
"What's the ruckus?"
"What's the racket?"
"What's the row?" yelled voices up and down the block.

Madame didn't notice the calico cats dangling from her hair. She didn't notice the plump, pecking pigeons. She didn't notice all the yelling. But she did hear the yowling.

"Mon Dieu!" she cried. "I hear singing. The opera must have started." Madame quickened her step.

Four French poodles out for their evening stroll heard the calico cats caught in Madame LaGrande's pompadour.

The poodles yipped.
The poodles yapped.
Their leashes snapped.
The four French poodles raced down the boulevard after the three calico cats caught in Madame LaGrande's pompadour.

"Foofoo!"
"Fifi!"
"Gigi!"
"Spot!" screamed the poodles' owners.

In her haste to get to the opera, Madame didn't notice the four French poodles following at her feet. She didn't notice the calico cats dangling from her pompadour. She didn't notice the plump, pecking pigeons. She noticed only that she was standing in front of the Royal Opera House and that the door was open.

The ceiling of the Opera House was so high Madame didn't have to bow her head to get inside. She swept in—yapping poodles, yowling cats, pecking pigeons, pompadour, and all.

The musicians stopped playing. The singers stopped singing. Everyone turned to stare at Madame LaGrande.

"Who dares to disturb the Royal Opera?" thundered the King, adjusting his monocle and leaning over the edge of his box for a closer look.

At that moment, Madame and her hair paraded by the King's box. The King's eyes widened in surprise. His monocle popped from his eye and plopped into the passing pompadour.

And the rest, as the French say, was history.

In a second, the King was yanked from his seat box. Wrapping his legs around the pompadour, he hugged it for dear life. The four French poodles sprang up and nipped at his heels. The three calico cats came uncaught and clawed up his back. The two plump pigeons flapped and perched, one on each of the King's shoulders. The audience gasped.

"It is breathtaking, isn't it?" agreed Madame LaGrande, who didn't notice the King clinging to her hair. Instead, she pulled out her compact to take a peek at her magnificent hairdo.

"Mon Dieu! My corkscrew curls have gone askew," cried
Madame. And she pulled out a tiny hairpin to fix the crooked curls.
The pompadour shivered.
The pompadour quivered.
The pompadour quaked.
"Avalanche!" cried the musicians.
"Hairslide!" cried the singers.
"TIMBER!" cried the audience.

Opera lovers scrambled over their seats, pushing and shoving to escape the falling pompadour. The pigeons took flight, alighting on the horned hat of the soprano on stage. The cats leapt off the King and into the orchestra pit. The poodles bounded after them.

Above the din came the shrill whistle of the Paris police as they burst into the Opera House. The four poodle owners followed closely behind.

"There she is!" pointed the fourth poodle's owner. "The one wearing the King."

The policemen dove for Madame LaGrande. But it was too late. Her pompadour exploded in a breathtaking display of wires and wigs, pillows and padding, flinging the King and his monocle clear across the Opera House. Luckily, the King landed on one of the hairdo's pillows, and nothing was hurt but the royal pride.

The King wrestled his way from beneath the hairdo's debris.
Sputtering with rage, he decreed, "Henceforth, all pompadours are
banned from the city of Paris!"

Then he fainted, the shock of being catapulted from a lady's
hairdo being too much for him. His royal guards carried him home.

Madame LaGrande returned home too, after straightening out her problems with the Paris police, sorting out the poodles, and shooing the cats and pigeons out the stage door. Then, after brushing her hair one hundred strokes, Madame relaxed in bed with her latest fashion magazine.

A story caught her eye. She read the story once. She read it twice. She sat straight up in bed. "Hoop skirts!" she exclaimed. "What a marvelous idea. I must call my dressmaker first thing in the morning. A hoop skirt would be très chic at the King's reception tomorrow night."